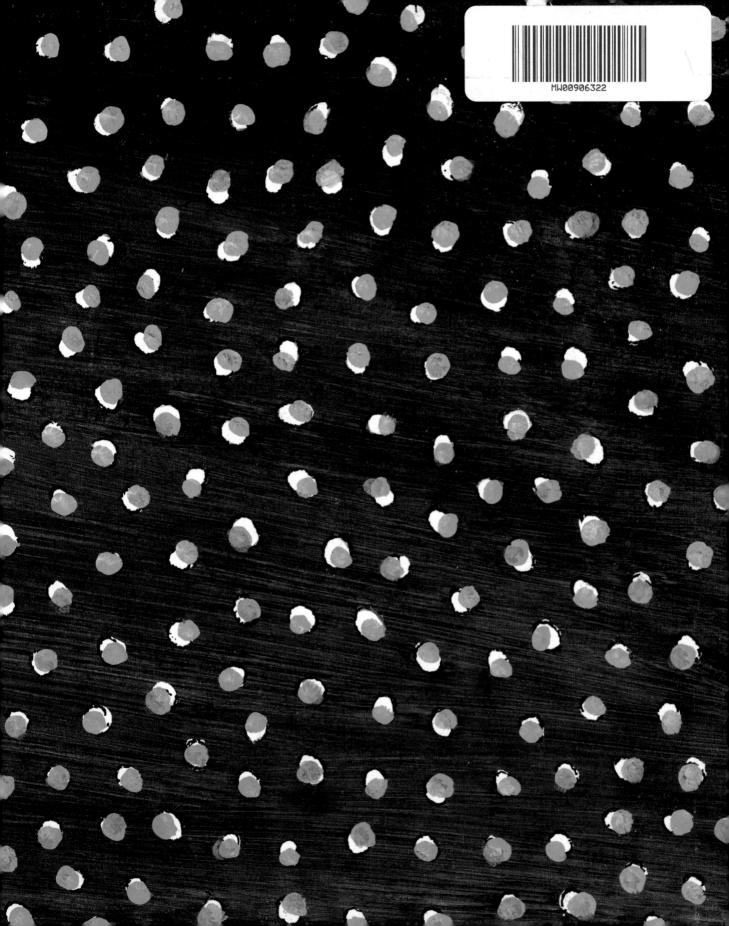

Isabelle Jossa

Ned goes to bed

SIMPLY READ BOOKS

Ned feels lonely when evening draws nigh,
Like the solitary moon in the dark blue sky.

Into his room, moonbeams creep
And Ned just cannot fall asleep.

He thinks that bedtime isn't rosy,
Even though his bed feels cozy.

Curled up safely under the covers,
Ned wonders what he might discover.

5, 4, 3, 2, 1
Time for liftoff
To the moon!

"Is anyone there?"
calls out Ned.

There was nothing but silence,
Not even a fly,
As the sun began its slow descent
Behind the earth's sky.

Then blackest night finally arrives
And loneliest Ned just wants to cry.

Don't worry, Ned, here we come!
We're Alpha, Capella and Orion.

Millions of bright stars began to appear,
Dancing with them everywhere.

Then in the magic of the constellations,
They plan a special celebration.

Enjoying themselves well and hearty,
Ned and friends have a cosmic party.

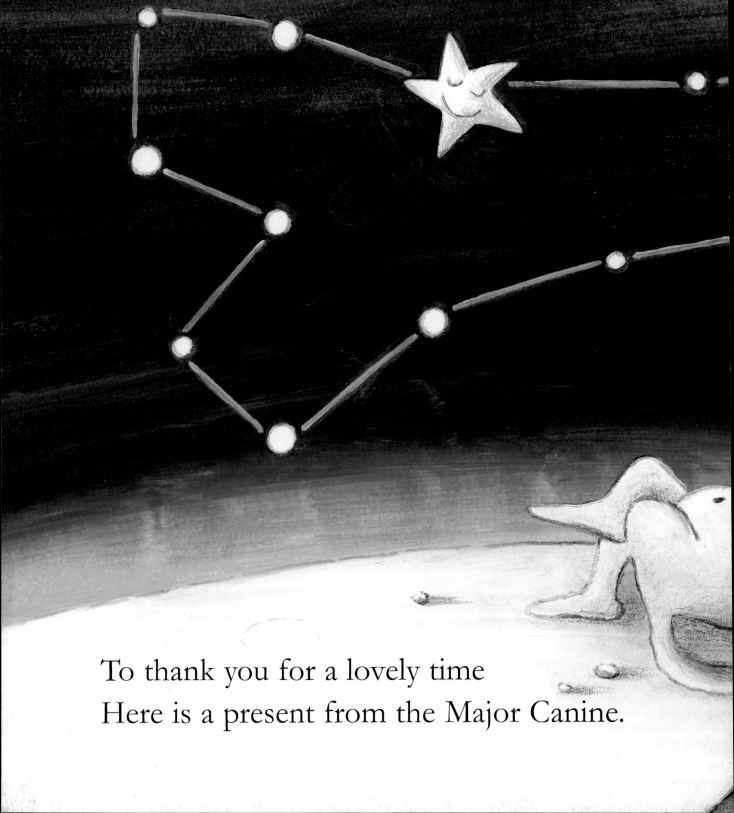

To thank you for a lovely time
Here is a present from the Major Canine.

Before the stars head across the sky
They take the time to say goodbye.

So long, good night, Ned. Go to bed.
Then Alpha, Capella and Orion make a wish,

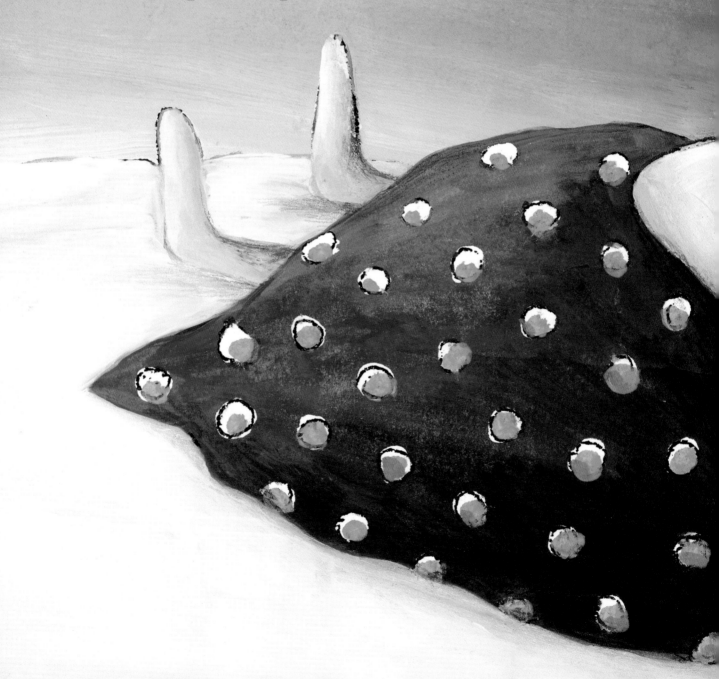

Sleep tight when you close your eyes at night,
And may all your stars be very bright.

Published in 2005 by Simply Read Books Inc. **www.simplyreadbooks.com**

Text and illustrations © 2005 by Isabelle Jossa
Translation © Elizabeth James

First published by Alice Éditions as *Agadir veut dormir*

CATALOGUING IN PUBLICATION DATA

Jossa, Isabelle, 1967-
    Ned goes to bed / Isabelle Jossa.
ISBN 1-894965-17-5

    I. Title.

PZ7.J78Ne 2005   j823   C2004-905676-X

10 9 8 7 6 5 4 3 2 1

PRINTED IN CHINA

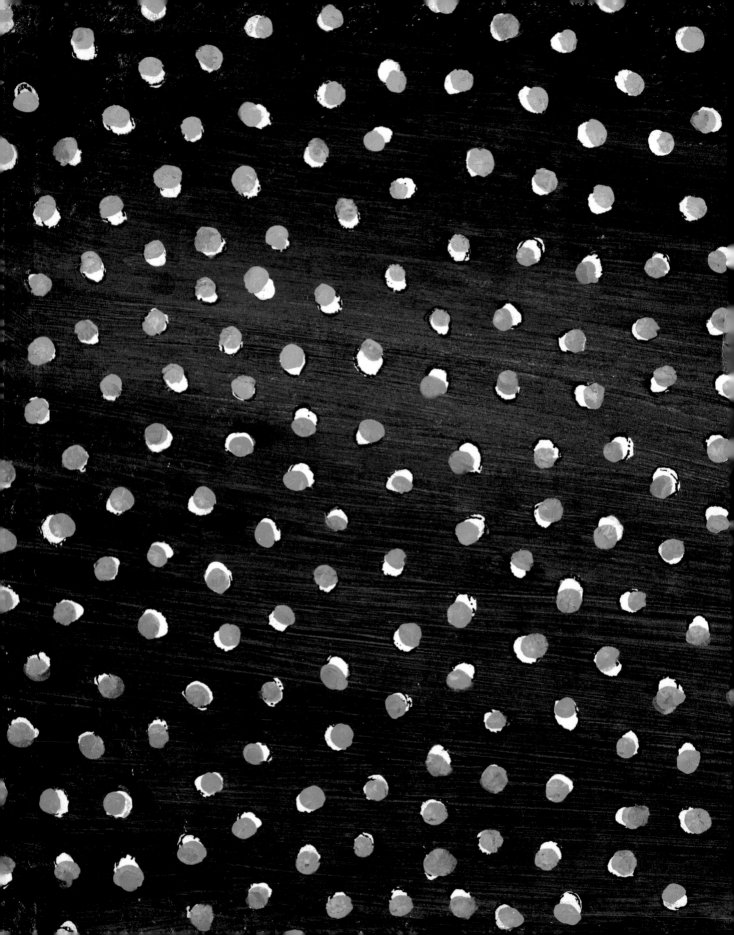